GW00866039

# THE GOOD THING
# ABOUT BAD DAYS

Child-friendly but deep. A great resource to help children cope well with difficult times and emotions. A book of excellent, easy to understand ideas that both help children to healthily express and manage their emotions and build resilience, and parents and carers to know how they can support them.

**SUE MONCKTON-RICKETT**
**Chair of the Association of Christian**
**Counsellors**

An imaginative treasure trove of ideas and activities, this insightful book helps young readers get through the ups and downs of their emotions.

**JOANNA BUGLASS**
**BSc (Hons) AdvDip (Counselling)**
**MBACP, professional counsellor**

This book will be another good thing about a bad day.

**HELEN HAY**
**BA (Hons) MA CQSW, social worker**

A warm and wise approach to the importance of nourishing a child's emotional health, and a useful resource for all those who care for children and young people.

**DR CLAIRE PARSONS**
**MB ChB, retired GP**

*The Good Thing About Bad Days* is a beautifully designed book. It explores the range and depth of mental discomfort that a young person may be going through and invites them to explore it in a safe and moderated way. Margaret McAllister's text is accessible and reassuring, Nigel Baines illustrations are age-appropriate, pertinent and inviting. The book is interactive and designed to allow a child the space for personal examination and expression. As a parent I would have found this book valuable simply as a framework for addressing mental stress that is both positive and healing. It is something I would certainly give to any struggling young person as a gift. It was written by a Christian and there are various references to faith, but these would not prevent someone of another faith, or of no faith, finding it helpful. Personal, powerful and professionally supported, this is a book with an approach that I think many parents, carers and children's practitioners will appreciate.

**KARENZA PASSMORE**
**Director of the North East Religious**
**Learning Resources Centre**

This book is heartwarming, funny, practical, real, and like a huge big hug. There is a Christian thread which runs throughout, but it is for everyone – of all faiths and none. Mental and spiritual health is so important and this book is a companion which can make us stronger, happier, and more peaceful with ourselves and others.

**REVD RACHEL SCHEFFER**
**Priest in Charge of Stamfordham, Matfen,**
**and Ryal, and Diocesan Development**
**Officer for Children's and Youth Work**

# THE GOOD THING ABOUT BAD DAYS

Margaret McAllister

Illustrated by Nigel Baines

LION
CHILDREN'S

Note: This book is written mostly for young readers.

However, if a book for young readers is any good, it can be enjoyed by everyone.

Parents, carers, and teachers might like to read it, too.

# CONTENTS

# BEFORE WE START

I hope you have good days – very many of them.

However, all of us have some bad days, and this book is to help you get through them. It's written in small sections because when you're unhappy you might not feel like anything bigger. There's also space for you to write or draw and fill in your own responses to help you through your bad days.

Let me introduce myself. I am Margi and I've raised three children and worked with children in all sorts of contexts, such as in churches as a volunteer. I've learned all I could along the way from being alongside children and observed how experts work with children, too.

I'm not the only one who wants you to be happy – so do most of the people in your life, and so do those who have helped me with this book. This book could not have been written without:

- Dr Claire Parsons MB ChB has just retired after nearly forty years as a general practice doctor. She has four sons. Claire has cared for everything from broken legs to broken hearts, troubled tummies and troubled minds, births, deaths, and everything in between.
- Helen Hay BA (Hons) MA CQSW is a social worker who has worked with hundreds of children with all sorts of needs, and has two children of her own.
- Joanna Buglass BSc (Hons) AdvDip (Counselling) MBACP is a professional counsellor and one of the wisest and most perceptive people I have ever met.

They are all exceptionally lovable, wise, kind, and altogether delightful. Like me, they want you to be happy, and that's why they've helped me to write this book.

I am a Christian, but I've tried to write this book so that it can be helpful to you, whatever you believe or don't believe. However, I find that if I sit down knowing that Jesus is with me and spend a bit of time with him, it always feels better.

The Lord is my shepherd;
I have everything I need.
He lets me rest in fields of green grass
and leads me to quiet pools of fresh water.

He gives me new strength.
He guides me in the right paths,
as he has promised.

Even if I go through the deepest darkness,
I will not be afraid, Lord,
for you are with me.
Your shepherd's rod and staff protect me.

*Psalm 23:1–4 [GNB]*

# BAD DAYS

## YOU MIGHT BE HAVING A BAD DAY FOR ANY OF THESE REASONS:

You've been disappointed. Perhaps you were looking forward to a special day and it isn't going to happen.

Something's worrying you and you don't know how to talk about it.

Nothing seems fair.

People are unkind to you.

There are days when everything goes wrong, including how you feel inside. There may be days when you can't seem to get anything right, however hard you try, and you're always in trouble. There may be days when you feel all wrong and mixed up inside and you can't do anything about it. Does that happen to you?

We're going to look at ways to cope with bad days. To begin with we'll use your thinking and your imagination because wherever you are, you have those with you.

First, I'll tell you something I used to tell my children. It's the good thing about bad days.

THE GOOD THING ABOUT BAD DAYS IS... THAT THEY COME TO AN END. THE BAD TIMES DON'T LAST FOR EVER.

# WHAT'S IN THE BOX?

## TIME TO USE YOUR IMAGINATION.

Imagine a box, a beautiful box that you might use for keeping jewels or treasures.

- IMAGINE EXACTLY WHAT IT LOOKS LIKE.
  - HOW BIG IS IT?
    - WHAT SHAPE?
      - WHAT COLOUR IS IT?
        - WHAT DOES IT FEEL LIKE?

CAREFULLY
OPEN THIS
BOX

Inside, you find the thing that's making you sad. Lift it out and put it down. It's still there, but you've put it to one side.

Now that you've moved it, you can see that all the good things in your life are in there, too! Hunt through and see what's in the box.

## THESE ARE SOME THINGS YOU MIGHT FIND IN THE BOX:

your closest friends, and all the people you love who love you too

a piece of music that makes you happy

a favourite toy – you might like to take it to bed

a favourite story – in a book or in your head

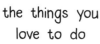

the things you love to do

your happiest memory

your favourite places

anything that makes you laugh: a joke, a picture, a story, a memory – anything!

All the good things in your life are in that box. These things will always help you feel better inside again.

**TRY THIS OUT** →

Choose something from the box that you really like. It might be a game you like to play or someone you want to spend time with. Maybe you'd like to write a story or make a picture. Lift the thing out of the box.

**1** IF IT'S SOMETHING TO DO, DO IT.

**2** IF IT'S SOMETHING TO MAKE, MAKE IT.

**3** IF IT'S SOMETHING TO THINK, THINK IT.

**4** IF IT'S SOMETHING TO SING, SING IT.

**5** IF IT'S SOMETHING (OR SOMEONE) TO HUG, HUG IT!

If you're in a place where you can't actually do this – maybe at school – then you can imagine doing it. But as soon as you can, sing your song, make your make, and give that hug.

You may find something in the box that you'd forgotten about. Imagine that perhaps, right at the bottom of the box or in a corner, there's a bead, a note, or a shell. Imagine this forgotten something is exactly what will help you to feel better.

REMEMBER

This box full of good things is inside you. You are full of good things!

Your heart will be where your treasure is.
*Matthew 6:21 [ICB]*

# WHAT DO YOU WANT TO KEEP IN YOUR IMAGINE BOX?

You might like to keep a list of the things in your box.

YOU MIGHT LIKE TO DRAW SOME OF THE THINGS IN YOUR BOX.

Some of the things I would put in my IMAGINE BOX are:

my family, my best friends, my godchildren, my happiest memories, roses, my favourite beach, sunny days by a lake, holidays, ducklings, monkeys, baby elephants, orangutans, my favourite books, babies, dancing, summer clothes, snow, autumn woods, and giggles.

As well as your IMAGINE BOX, you could keep a box of real things to make you feel better. Find a box – it could be an unused shoebox or cardboard box. You could decorate the box.

In this box, you could keep anything that makes you say, "Isn't that wonderful!" Collect things like shells, petals, leaves, or anything that makes you gasp at how beautifully and perfectly it's made.

What might you keep in this box? If you can't get the real thing, a picture of it will help.

By the way, you have a completely amazing nose. It keeps you alive doing all that breathing, even when you're asleep. Your nose is always with you. (Or I hope it is!)

 I praise you because you made me in an amazing and wonderful way. What you have done is wonderful. I know this very well.

*Psalm 139:14 [ICB]*

# WHAT WOULD YOU PUT IN YOUR REAL BOX?

You might like to keep a list of the things that you'll find to put in your box.

In my REAL BOX I would keep some of my favourite shells, things my children have made, one or two books, photographs, a spinning top, a tiny jigsaw, my grandmother's birthday book, and a parrot brooch that Dr Claire gave me when she knew I needed something to make me laugh.

## REMEMBER

On bad days, keep asking – what else is in the box to help you feel better?

# WHEN YOU FEEL ANGRY OR SAD

Do you sometimes feel angry? Of course you do. We all do.

Angry feelings can make us sad, too, and make us do things we shouldn't, so it's good to know how to deal with them.

If you know why you feel angry, it helps if you can explain it to somebody who will be patient and will try to understand. If it's hard to find the words, you could draw a picture to show to someone you trust.

## YOU MIGHT LIKE TO TRY THIS:

Imagine your feelings as an angry little person. Talk to that person kindly, as you would to a frightened animal. (You can talk to sad and grumpy feelings like that, too).

Then, when you've talked to your feelings, do something completely different.

## YOU COULD:

**1** Get moving. Run until you're breathless, play a ball game, or dance yourself exhausted.

**2** Do something kind. Make somebody a card, or be really helpful. Being kind can make you feel a lot better.

**3** Find something funny, the funnier the better – something that can make you laugh even if you didn't mean to. Have you ever tried to be grumpy and giggly at the same time? It's not easy!

There are some things that I find naturally funny, like false teeth, tongue twisters, rude noises, cats chasing their tails, ducks waddling, and words like poodle, noodle, doodle, and hollyhock. I keep those in my IMAGINE BOX. What about you?

# SOMETIMES WE'RE TOO SAD OR TOO ANGRY TO THINK OF ANYTHING HAPPY.

**REMEMBER**

At night, and on cloudy days, you can't see the sunshine. But that doesn't mean there isn't any sun, does it? The sun is still there. It will come out again. Happiness is like that. It may have disappeared now, but you will be happy again.

I could say, "The darkness will hide me.
The light around me will turn into night."
But even the darkness is not dark to you.
The night is as light as the day.
Darkness and light are the same to you.

*Psalm 139:11–12 [ICB]*

## SAD THINGS HAPPEN, AND SOMETIMES WE CAN'T UNDERSTAND WHY THEY HAPPEN.

A time comes when it's best to stop trying to make sense of it all. Worrying only makes us feel worse. Even when we can't understand, we can help each other through.

**REMEMBER**

In your life you will meet people who like you, love you, and support you. And you can become a kind, caring person yourself. You can have good friends and be a good friend to them, too.

Who are the kind, helpful people in your life? You might like to draw them.

 "Who needs me to love them today?" This is something Dr Claire says. When you're feeling sad, see if you can help somebody else who is sad. You'll both feel better for it.

## TRY THIS:

When sad things happen, you might feel as if you're carrying your sadness around with you. It gets heavy. Imagine it as a suitcase full of bricks!

Now imagine putting that suitcase down and going away. Leave the suitcase behind. It is probably for somebody else to sort out anyway, not you.


## OR TRY THIS:

If you have a pet, you might try telling your sad things to them. Or you might tell the sad things to a favourite toy. Putting things into words and saying them out loud might make you feel better. After you've told a pet or a toy, you've found a way of talking about it, which will help if, later, you need to tell a person. We'll think about doing that soon.

If you feel that it will never get better, think of a caterpillar that becomes a chrysalis and then turns into a butterfly. When it's a chrysalis, it probably doesn't feel much like a butterfly – but that's what it will be! You may feel as if you will never be happy again, but you will.

Once when I was feeling very, very low, my son texted me and asked me how he could help. I wrote, "Tell me something funny." He replied, "Mr Squeakle likes to sleep on the toilet." It turned out that Mr Squeakle was one of the guinea pigs he was looking after for a friend. Mr Squeakle fell asleep in the poo corner. If a giggle would help, think of Mr Squeakle.

REMEMBER

IT WILL GET BETTER.

What's the good thing about bad days? They come to an end.

# IT'S NOT FAIR!

## SOMETIMES, LIFE IS FAIR.

You work hard on a school project and get good marks. You and your friends all get the same amount of pocket money and get similar birthday presents.

Sometimes, life is fairer than it looks. Maybe your friend gets lots more pocket money than you, but he has to pay for his clothes out of it – and you don't. Or your brother gets more computer time than you do, but he's older and needs it for his homework. We don't always know whether things are fair or not.

But sometimes – because the world isn't perfect and neither are we, things are just not fair.

## LIFE WON'T ALWAYS BE FAIR.

That doesn't mean that we should just let unfairness go on. We all have to make everything as fair as we can. But sometimes, when things are unfair, we can't change them. We can't do anything about the unfairness, but we can do something about our own feelings.

It's all right to feel angry about unfairness. But letting that anger become the biggest thing in your life doesn't help. Don't let anger blot out the good things.

REMEMBER

What are the good things in your box? Look again at your ideas (on pages 14 and 15) and see what helps you feel better.

Then your goodness will shine like the sun.
Your fairness will shine like the noonday sun.

*Psalm 37:6 [ICB]*

# WHEN YOU FEEL BAD ABOUT SOMETHING YOU'VE DONE

EVERYONE

 EVERYONE

 EVERYONE

MAKES
MISTAKES.

I make mistakes, and so do you. None of us get everything right the first time. Sometimes making mistakes is the only way that we can learn.

If you've done something you shouldn't, try this:

be sorry

SORRY

make things better
if you can

- and then take a deep breath and start again. You're not a bad person. You just got something wrong. Try not to do it again!

26

# AND ASK YOURSELF, WHAT ELSE IS IN THE BOX?

What will you use from your IMAGINE BOX to remind you that good things are inside you?

REMEMBER

It'll be all right. The sun will still come up in the morning.

I told God everything:
I told God about all the wrong things I had done.

I gave up trying to pretend.
I gave up trying to hide.

I knew that the only thing to do was to say sorry.
And God forgave me.

*Based on Psalm 32:5*

# SOME GOOD THINGS TO TURN AROUND BAD THOUGHTS

## ALL KINDS OF THOUGHTS COME INTO OUR HEADS.

Some of them may be thoughts that we don't like. We don't mean to think them, they just turn up in our heads anyway. They upset us.

You might find yourself thinking of frightening things. They are just thoughts. They don't mean that anything bad is going to happen. Imagine yourself getting rid of these things, like throwing them in a rubbish bin, looking the other way, and holding your nose as if they're something smelly. Leave them there and do something that makes you happy.

## YOU MAY THINK OF DOING SAD OR BAD THINGS.

It doesn't mean that you are bad, or that you will do anything bad. They are only thoughts, that's all, and you needn't worry about them.

You could imagine opening a window in your head and letting them fly out! Or you might think of them like bubbles that burst. You could even blow some bubbles and pop them, and imagine that you've popped the bad thoughts.

REMEMBER

What else is in your box to help you feel better?

# WORRY, AND WHY YOU DON'T NEED TO

## MAYBE YOU WORRY ABOUT THINGS.

Worry is like a magnifying glass that makes things look a lot bigger than they really are.

You might have a problem that is really only this big...

...but worrying makes it look like THIS...

...OR EVEN LIKE THIS, WITH BIG TEETH!

But it can be sorted out. You don't have to do it all on your own.

Imagine the worry as the suitcase full of bricks that I told you about (on page 22). Now imagine putting it down so that you can go away and do something you like.

Worrying about things won't change them. The best thing is to find somebody you can trust and tell them what worries you. Further on in this book, we'll think about who to tell.

If there's nobody there who can help you, tell your worries to your pet or a favourite toy. Or you could open a window and let the worries fly out. Or blow some bubbles and blow the worries away, or pop them.

You don't have to drag your worries around with you. They won't do you any good!

Sometimes it's hard to talk about our worries because we think, "I can't tell anybody that..." Read on.

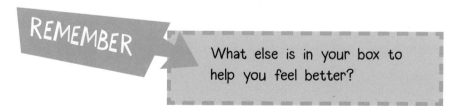

REMEMBER

What else is in your box to help you feel better?

Leave all your worries with him, because he cares for you.
*1 Peter 5:7 [GNB]*

# I CAN'T TELL ANYBODY THAT!

You might have a problem so difficult, so troubling, or so embarrassing that you think it has never happened to anyone before. You might think you couldn't possibly talk about that.

## THIS IS WHAT YOU NEED TO KNOW.

The world has been here for a long time! You may think that your problem is so strange, so bad, or so terrible that it has never happened to anyone else before.

Well, it has.

Somebody has been through this before you. Lots of people, most likely.

## THERE IS HELP FOR YOU.

I know that some things are hard enough to go through without having to talk about them as well. It isn't easy, is it? You might feel you don't want to think about your problem, let alone talk about it. But talking is the thing that will help. The important thing is to talk to the right person.

Remember what we were thinking about on page 29. You might like to practise talking to a favourite toy or a pet first.

Choose very carefully who you tell. We're going to look at that next.

Remember what we were thinking about on page 29.

## REMEMBER

There are people who can help you. Life is good, even if it doesn't feel that way right now.

# HELP! TELLING AND SHARING

If somebody or something is upsetting you and you can't sort it out for yourself, tell someone.

## CHOOSE VERY CAREFULLY WHO YOU TELL.

It might be one of your parents, or a grandparent, or auntie, or uncle.

If there's nobody in your family you feel you can talk to, what about one of your teachers? They're not there just to give lessons. They are there to help you! If you are in a faith community, you might like to talk to one of the leaders or youth workers. If you go to any clubs, or something like Brownies, Guides, Cubs, or Scouts, the leader might be somebody you can talk to.

# ASK YOURSELF THESE QUESTIONS:

WHO DO I FEEL SAFE WITH?

WHO WON'T LAUGH AT ME OR TELL ME NOT TO BE SILLY?

WHO HAS HELPED ME BEFORE?

WHO CAN I TRUST?

Imagine talking to a person who will make space and time for you, listen patiently and carefully, and understand that this is hard for you to talk about. Who might this be?

Most things can be sorted out by sharing them with a trusted adult. If you do need more than that, they can put you in touch with an expert on helping children and young people with their problems. Yes, there are such people and they want to help you.

Even with your trusted person, you might find it really hard to talk about the thing that's bothering you. It's normal to feel like that. And you might find it easiest to talk to your trusted person while you're busy doing something together – maybe washing up, or a jigsaw or some other kind of puzzle. If you're talking to a parent or godparent, or perhaps an auntie, long walks and drives are good times for talking, too.

If you can't find anyone else to tell, there's Childline. You can call them on 0800 1111 and it doesn't cost anything. It won't even show on the phone bill that you've called them. The person at the other end of the phone is trained to help you. That's what Childline does. Their advisers are people who want you to enjoy your life!

REMEMBER

There is help for you. You can get through this.

God is our shelter and strength,
always ready to help in times of trouble.

*Psalm 46:1 [GNB]*

# NOBODY HAS THE RIGHT TO SPOIL YOUR LIFE

What if somebody is upsetting you and you can't stop them?
This is one of those times when you absolutely must get help.

**REMEMBER**

NOBODY has the right to make you unhappy.
NOBODY has the right to spoil your life.
YOU ARE WORTH MORE THAN THAT.

But I said I wouldn't tell.

## THIS IS IMPORTANT:

If somebody makes you promise to do something you feel
you shouldn't, you don't have to keep that promise. It's more
important to get out of that situation. Tell your trusted person.

It's the same if somebody asks you to keep a secret.
If you feel that it's a bad secret and you shouldn't keep it,
then you don't have to. Again, tell the person you trust.

The sooner you tell, the better. Telling somebody you trust is like handing the suitcase full of worry to somebody really strong who can handle it, smash it up with a hammer, or heave it out of the window.

Bullies often warn you not to tell on them. That's because they're afraid of what will happen to them if you do.

   If someone is making you unhappy, and you tell, and nothing changes – go on telling. Don't pretend it's all right if it isn't.

And if anyone tells you you're horrible, ugly or stupid – well, they're wrong! There's a lot to like about you!

Write down three things you like about yourself. More, if you like. Remember, there is nobody else in the world quite like you. The world is a better place because you are in it.

Here are three things I like about myself:

I'M GOOD AT WRITING STUFF.
I MAKE PEOPLE LAUGH.
I'M HELPFUL.

1

2

3

# AT THE END OF THE DAY
## (OR ANY TIME YOU LIKE, IF YOU NEED IT)

Before you go to bed, think of the day you've had. Even if you've had a bad day, there will be something good in there for you to think about. You may have to think hard to remember what it was. It might just be saying hello to a cat on your way home from school, or a cartoon that made you laugh. On good days – and there will always be good days – you'll have lots of happy memories to enjoy. So at bedtime, ask yourself:

What was the nicest part of my day?

Think of something lovely before you go to sleep. When my children were young, I used to say to them, "Pink ice creams!" It started off as "Think nice dreams!", but somewhere along the way we turned it into "pink ice creams", which means the same thing. You may prefer purple, green, or stripy ice creams. Colour this ice cream however you like.

 Finally, brothers and sisters, whatever is true, whatever is noble, whatever is right, whatever is pure, whatever is lovely, whatever is admirable – if anything is excellent or praiseworthy – think about such things.

*Philippians 4:8 [NIV]*

I hope you don't have many sad times – but when sad times come, I hope you can come to this book and find something that helps you with it. And I hope that you find your own ways of helping you through bad days, and helping your friends and family through theirs.

REMEMBER

Being kind helps you feel better. You might like to use the end of this book as a notebook where you write down the things that help you.

REMEMBER

What's the good thing about bad days? They come to an end! This too will pass.

# YOUR NOTEBOOK

These are your pages to note down or draw how you are feeling, or plan how to tell someone you trust how you are feeling. What good things from your IMAGINE BOX or REAL BOX can help you feel better?

Come to me, all of you who are tired and have heavy loads. I will give you rest.

*Matthew 11:28 [ICB]*

So don't worry, because I am with you.
Don't be afraid, because I am your God.
I will make you strong and will help you.
I will support you with my right hand
that saves you.

*Isaiah 41:10 [ICB]*

But those who trust in the Lord for help
will find their strength renewed.
They will rise on wings like eagles;
they will run and not get weary;
they will walk and not grow weak.

*Isaiah 40:31 [GNB]*

The Lord will protect you
from all danger;
he will keep you safe.
He will protect you as you
come and go
now and for ever.

*Psalm 121:7–8 [GNB]*

# FOR PARENTS AND CARERS

## WRITTEN BY DR CLAIRE PARSONS

## A CHILD I CARE ABOUT IS HAVING A BAD DAY. HOW WOULD I KNOW, AND WHAT CAN I DO?

It is a fact of life that everybody is likely to encounter difficulties, challenges, setbacks, or sadness at some point in their life, and unfortunately, children and young people are not immune from this. It may just be a "bad day" when nothing seems to be going right, or there may be some deeper, more prolonged difficulty affecting that child's happiness and well-being. Children can suffer from depression, anxiety, and fears just like adults, and they too may have to cope with bereavement, loss, relationship difficulties, unrealized hopes and dreams, and unfair treatment as they learn and grow.

### HOW WOULD I KNOW?

Parents and carers in close contact with a child quickly become "specialists" regarding that child, being in the best position by their daily interaction to observe their behaviour, recognize their emerging personality, and be attentive to their needs. Therefore they are most likely to be able to recognize their child's distress. Just as new parents rapidly learn to identify a baby's "hungry" cry, as opposed to its "I need changing"/ "I'm bored"/ "I want you to pick me up" cry. It is likely that you will be able to recognize the difference between the sort of "bad day" feeling that can be helped by a listening ear, a cuddle, and commiseration, and a more serious difficulty.

Knowing a bit about how children develop, and at what age it might be reasonable to expect certain behaviours – for example, why people refer to the "terrible twos" and toddler tantrums – can be very helpful. All children are individuals, and have their own "normal", though, so we have to be flexible in our expectations.

### WHAT CAN I DO?

As a parent or carer your instinct is to want to shield your children from danger and unhappiness. The mildest person may become a tiger in defence of their child! It is a hard, sometimes heartbreaking, moment when you realize that you can't always protect them from hurt or disappointment. However, there is a lot you can do to help equip them with the strategies they need to deal with life, to recognize when they are distressed, and to enable them to find ways of coping, and moving on from their bad days.

Getting into the habit of spending a few moments each day sharing what has been good or sometimes not so good about your day and theirs with your children can help teach them to recognize and express their feelings, and to trust that they can tell you how they feel. Sharing your joys and sorrows, and finding that even on bad days good things can happen, helps them learn an ability to see things in proportion and develop resilience.

Learning that they can talk to you about their feelings, even negative or angry feelings, without criticism or your needing to "make it better" can be really valuable to help them move on from whatever has upset them and made that day bad for them.

Stories of many kinds can be a great way of communicating, and a child can find both comfort and inspiration from them. There are some excellent books now, even for very young children, that talk about emotions, but any bedtime stories, tales from faith traditions, and familiar "fairy tales" can be a good launching point to discuss feelings. (Any toddler having to cope with a new baby in the family might identify with Baby Bear's plaintive cry of "Who's been sleeping in *my* bed?" in *Goldilocks and the Three Bears*!).

Observing how your child plays, whether on their own or with others, and learning what seems to bring them comfort or distress can be really useful.

Playing with them yourself – perhaps a simple matching or board game – can help a child learn how to take turns, how to cope with being a "winner" or "loser" in small ways, and can be great fun for you both.

In this technological age, it is important to be aware of other influences that may impact on your child – for instance, being aware of what they might see on television or a computer – so encouraging them to be able to talk to you about things they might find upsetting or strange is a good habit to form.

## SIGNS OF DEEPER CONCERN

If a child seems persistently unhappy, withdrawn, or angry (and "bad" behaviour can be an indicator of fear, anxiety, and low self-esteem, rather than a child having a "bad" temperament or personality), that suggests something is troubling them, and that is when they need you most. They need you to notice and care. Perhaps they can only express their frustration by breaking things or lashing out, maybe they are punishing themselves by refusing to eat, or seeming to deliberately provoke you. Even very young children have been known to self-harm, by scratching themselves, headbanging, or pulling their hair out. Try to look beyond the distressing behaviour to the well-being of the child, and keep telling them you love them even when you really don't feel that you like them at that moment! If things are tough and you feel outside help is needed, don't be afraid to look for it.

Sometimes, when whatever is causing a child distress is more than just a temporary problem, keeping them safe and enabling positive change for your child may involve seeking "specialist" help – this could be a doctor, health visitor, family therapist, granny, psychologist, or teacher. ALWAYS seek help if you suspect the child may be being subjected to abuse of any kind. Asking for assistance for your child doesn't mean you have failed in any way. Your unconditional love and support for them, and your willingness to find the resources they need, are essential.

## REFLECTIONS

Here are a few things that you might find it useful to think about, and a list of some books and resources.

This list is not exhaustive. Maybe you can think of things you would like to add or change?

Be aware that you need most of these things too. If you are exhausted, isolated, grieving, worrying about finances, or experiencing health or emotional difficulties yourself, it may be harder to identify what may be affecting your child and to be able to support them. Being a parent or primary carer is an extremely hard job, and unfortunately taking on the role does not automatically equip you with superpowers! What support networks or resilience-building activities are possible for you?

## What every child needs and deserves

- Basic care: providing food, clothing, shelter, and cleanliness
- Love
- Emotional warmth: providing affection and approval
- Stability: providing security, and the opportunity to make lasting attachments with carers
- Stimulation: providing a balance between this, and the opportunity to relax and be quiet
- Interest
- Need recognition
- Guidance: providing appropriate boundaries and learning self-control
- "Starting point" for a child: providing nurturing, opportunities, and encouragement so that the child can develop healthy self-esteem and the skills to be independent eventually

## Books and resources
(Many others are available, and accessible online and in bookshops and libraries.)

* Exploring Feelings: Cognitive Behaviour Therapy to Manage Anxiety by Dr Tony Atwood
Future Horizons Inc.
ISBN 978 1 932565 22 5

* *Happy Hippo, Angry Duck:*
*A Book of Moods*
by Sandra Boynton
Little Simon.
ISBN 978 1 4424 1731 1

* *The Huge Bag of Worries*
by Virginia Ironside and Frank Rodgers
Hodder Children's Books.
ISBN 978 0 340 90317 9

* *A Volcano in My Tummy:*
*Helping Children to Handle Anger*
by Eliane Whitehouse and Warwick
Pudney
New Society Publishers.
ISBN 978 0 86571 349 9

* *When My Worries Get Too Big!*
*A Relaxation Book for Children*
*Who Live with Anxiety*
by Karl Dunn Buron
AAPC Publishing.
ISBN 978 1 937473 80 8

**Care For The Family**:
www.careforthefamily.org.uk

**Childline:**
0800 1111 or online advice and help
www.childline.org.uk

**The Children's Society**:
www.childrenssociety.org.uk

**Family Line**:
familyline@family-action.org.uk
www.family-action.org.uk

**Mind** – mental health charity that
provides information about where
children and young people can access
help with mental health problems:
www.mind.org.uk/information-support/
guides-to-support-and-services/
children-and-young-people

**NSPCC**:
www.nspcc.org.uk

**Samaritans**:
116 123 (UK)
www.samaritans.org

**YoungMinds Parents Helpline**:
0808 802 5544 (UK)
(free calls Mon–Fri 9:30 a.m.–4 p.m.)
www.youngminds.org.uk

Remember, if you have concerns about
a child being at risk of any kind of abuse
(physical, emotional, sexual, or neglect),
it is vital to report your concerns as
soon as possible. This can be to the
police, social services, your family
doctor, or a school or nursery – all
these organizations have safeguarding
guidelines, and can help you.

*Picture books by Lion Hudson*
*to help you talk about issues*

*Are You Sad, Little Bear?*
by Rachel Rivett and Tina Macnaughton
– about bereavement.
ISBN 978 0 7459 6430 0

*Hogs Hate Hugs!*
by Tiziana and John Brendall-Brunello
– about family and independence.
ISBN 978 0 7459 6483 6

*I Want a Friend*
by Anne Booth and Amy Proud
– about friendship.
ISBN 978 0 7459 7706 5

*Just Because*
by Rebecca Elliott
– about disability.
ISBN 978 0 7459 6235 1

*Just Like You*
by Sarah J. Dodd and Giusi Capizzi
– about friendship.
ISBN 978 0 7459 7713 3

*Legs*
by Sarah J. Dodd and Giusi Capizzi
– about family and independence.
ISBN 978 0 7459 6598 7

*Magnus*
by Claire Shorrock
– about acceptance and diversity.
ISBN 978 0 7459 6573 4

*Missing Jack*
by Rebecca Elliott
– about bereavement.
ISBN 978 0 7459 6578 9

*The Sheep in Wolf's Clothing*
by Bob Hartman and Tim Raglin
– about acceptance and diversity.
ISBN 978 0 7459 6500 0

Text copyright © 2020 Margaret McAllister
Illustrations by Nigel Baines
This edition copyright © 2020 Lion Hudson IP Limited

The right of Margaret McAllister to be identified as
the author of this work has been asserted by her in
accordance with the Copyright, Designs and Patents
Act 1988.

All rights reserved. No part of this publication may
be reproduced or transmitted in any form or by any
means, electronic or mechanical, including photocopy,
recording, or any information storage and retrieval
system, without permission in writing from the
publisher.

Published by
**Lion Hudson Limited**
Wilkinson House, Jordan Hill Business Park,
Banbury Road, Oxford OX2 8DR, England
www.lionhudson.com

ISBN 978 0 7459 7844 4

First edition 2020

**Acknowledgements**
Scriptures quotations marked [GNB] are taken from
the Good News Bible © 1994 published by the Bible
Societies/HarperCollins Publishers Ltd UK, Good
News Bible© American Bible Society 1966, 1971, 1976,
1992. Used with permission.
Scriptures quotations marked [ICB] are taken from The
Holy Bible, International Children's Bible® Copyright©
1986, 1988, 1999, 2015 by Tommy Nelson™, a division
of Thomas Nelson. Used by permission.
Scripture quotations marked [NIV] are taken from
the Holy Bible, New International Version Anglicised.
Copyright ⊠ 1979, 1984, 2011 Biblica, formerly
International Bible Society. Used by permission of
Hodder & Stoughton Ltd, an Hachette UK company.
All rights reserved. "NIV" is a registered trademark of
Biblica. UK trademark number 1448790.

A catalogue record for this book is available from the
British Library

Printed and bound in China, February 2020, LH54